inside pale eyes

inside pale eyes

Dave Ward

inside
pale
eyes

A fractured narrative of grey twilight where half-glimpsed figures flicker through a deserted city-scape. Connection is everything, but nobody connects.

Midnight Max straddles time on his all-night radio station; Skin slashes chords from a ghost guitar trapped inside his tower block while, out in the night, trucks roar and hammer, taxis swoop and cruise, and slow cars drift through shadowy mist.

The dim eyes of streetlamps watch the eyes which watch each other sizing up their moves, languid as decay, sudden as disease.

Text by DAVE WARD
Drawings by BRYAN BIGGS

inside pale eyes

Text©2019 Dave Ward
Drawings©2019 Bryan Biggs

ISBN 978-908577-85-6

5 3 1 2 4
First Edition

All rights reserved

British Library Cataloguing in Publication Data.
A catalogue record for this book is available from
the British Library.

Conditions of Sale
No part of this book may be reproduced or transmitted by
any means without the permission of the publisher.

This is a work of fiction. Any reference to persons, living or
dead, is purely coincidental.

Hawkwood Books 2019

Acknowledgements

These pieces were first written in 1980s/90s when some appeared in

> Ambit
> The Brobdingnagian Times
> Flux
> Global Tapestry
> Greedy Pigs
> I Hate The World (Sweden)
> The Interpreter's House
> Lateral Moves
> Oasis
> Renegade
> Slacker
> Splizz.

This is the first time they have been collected together.

- 1 -

A woman holds out her baby. She asks for change, for milk, for clothes. Nothing changes. The baby does not know. She sleeps at peace in her mother's outstretched arms. The baby knows everything.

Waking, she sees the scornful faces, the pitying faces, the pitiful faces, the faceless faces that turn away, that lurch towards her. The eyes that pry, that pierce, that do not realise they see.

The baby screams. She needs changing. Her mother pleads for change. Her mother screams. The baby holds her in her arms. They hold each other. The scream is one. There is no change.

The endless rain. Grey faces, grey streets, a sullen river of endless pain. The walls of the cathedral hug them close as motherhood. The walls are harsh.

A harsh grey stone.

The baby feels the pain is feeding her. Unyielding hunger. Her mother pleads again. There is no change. Only hunger. Only rain.

- 2 -

In a tower block no-one can hear you scream. And even if they do, no-one knows where it's coming from as the sound ghosts around the girders, flickers from floor to floor. But if you're the only one living there that owns a Stratocaster, they come down straight away, clattering and complaining to your door.

Skin rams home the jack and runs his fingers across the fretboard to unlock the riff that aches inside him, then sits back and waits to see who will knock first. The guitar's taut strings sing a whispering echo. Nobody comes.

No-one was listening. Nobody cares.

He plugs the radio back in and slashes the deejay's smoky voice with silent frenzied chords.

- 3 -

As midnight hits, Max sits in the radio station's one-eyed shack. His mouth is dry, his temples throb. Every night it's the same. He watches the clock, watches the second hand sweep towards the top – right on time, right on cue. That invisible moment as one day chases into the next. Max straddles time, opens his line, whispers grit and velvet down the throat of the microphone then flips a switch and yawns, that long drag of air fed by knotted nerves. As the rhythm of the first track down cracks the channels, Max relaxes, grins and unwinds. His head stops beating as he drains a glass of pure ice water. From now on in he wire-walks each sweet moment.

Out in the night, trucks roar and hammer, taxis swoop and cruise. Max keeps on feeding them the rhythm and the blues. Booze flows from bottle to glass to gullet to hot sizzling piss in the shabeens and parties, back alleys and bedsits, back kitchens and flop houses strewn across town. Max scores the soundtrack to a movie he never sees as the long hours drift into the all-night shift, breaking the sounds as the city sleeps, the dreamers wake, the ravers dream.

"For all you lonely lovers and all you loving loners, this is where you get connected. Just pick up the phone."

Max opens the line. Dead air.

"Is there somebody there? Talk to me. Talk..."

A muffled sobbing. Then Max's words echo back to him. A woman's voice.

"Is there somebody there?"

She's crying now. Hot tears well in the mouthpiece of the phone.

"Talk to me..."

The words and the tears feeding back down the lines. The radio is on in her room, but all that she hears is her own voice spilling out again. All the pain echoing round and round. Building into a howl of electric sound.

"Talk..."

- 4 -

Albie sticks his mop back in the bucket. The dirty water slops over the top, splashes across his boots. He wants to wash his hands again. Sighs. The sign above his head tells him he's on the seventh floor. Seven floors down to his cubby hole in the entrance hall. Seven floors up to his flat at the top. Here he is on the middle floor of the middle block of the towers that glower like look-out posts at the edge of the estate.

Below him the concrete stairs still steam where he's wiped the balding mop across them. Above him the smell of dog piss, vomit and god knows what.

It makes him feel dirty. He wants to wash his hands. Rubs them on the back of his overalls. He could knock on a door and ask to use a bathroom. But then it would be - "Albie, have you come to fix the sink?" Or - "Albie, where'd you get to yesterday when I got stuck in the lift?"

He flicks at an empty aerosol can, spent on graffiti that no-one will read, here in the dankness of no-man's land. A shadowy desert of concrete and brick. Water, water everywhere. He can hear it trickle and drip.

He wants to wash his hands. A door bangs somewhere above him. The wind whines ghostly through the lift-shaft's creaking cables. Slowly, he takes off his gloves. Dips his hands into the mop-bucket's turgid water, wringing them gently, like a cloth. Then he draws them out, shakes them, wipes them again, across the back of his overalls.

From somewhere below, somewhere above, Skin is tuning his guitar. The sound slips and slithers like liquid lightning along the gridwork of girders that is the skeleton of the block.

Albie waits for his hands to dry before pulling the gloves back on. As he heaves the bucket up the next flight of stairs, the water with its tang of bleach and detergent that masks the smell of piss, sloshes out across his boots again.

He wants to wash his hands.

- 5 -

"Chasing shadows, chasing dreams – it seems that's all we do these days... What are we anyway? Only the children of shadows ourselves... Shadows of shadows. Shadows of dreams."

Skin watches the flow of the old man's hands.

"But in the dreams we become what it is we want to be. We sing. Let me sing this to you."

He opens up one moon eye, wild. And seizing Skin's wrist, spits a gob of phlegm into his outstretched palm.

"What's this? We start from something that looks like this. Feels like this. Stick your finger there and tell me. What's the difference? And we're filled with this. Just bags of snot and blood. But aren't we beautiful, eh? Aren't we lovely? See how we dance."

Beside a battered suitcase in the middle of a mud-filled park, the old man stands up. Skin backs off as he extends an arm, groping towards his shoulder, but then the old man stumbles and crashes, a perished balloon collapsing, face down in the slime.

- 6 -

"What do you think about the situation?"

His moon face sways pudgily. The shot eyes blink a deceptive innocence. He has lumbered uncertainly the length of the street to get this far, negotiating corners, cars and kerbs with slow deliberation. Perched on his head the pelt of a teddy bear slit open, ripped, its guts spilt to the wind, hunting trophy hat prized from a bin.

She pivots a pirouette. Twirls the stick and drops it. Twirls the stick and drops it. Standing in the rain kissing lipstick. A grown woman playing young girls' games. Her skirt hitched up as she curses the buses.

He lurches closer, his grubby raincoat undone to show where his flies hang casually open, as if no-one would notice. Knowing everyone will.

She'd seen him before, sat grinning at the crossroads, waving smiling flowers at the sullen buses. But suddenly close up he's menacingly serious. No joking, no laughs. The makeshift hat slips across his face as he repeats in a muted high pitch:

"What do you think about the situation?"

Her stick clatters once again onto the pavement. Cats-eye glasses slither down her nose as she bends to pick it up, her other hand yanking back a hank of uncombed hair.

In the air, above the roofs, below the clouds, a swirl of seagulls swoop and dive, and in their own torn raucous voices, sing.

- 7 -

In the grim ghostyard Max sees the creatures move. Only at dusk. Only at dawn. Shadowy mechanical marionettes trapped out of time between these walls.

He wonders who is really out of place as he sits entwined in his electric maze, cat's cradle of wires and cables, clutter of discs and tapes. Stereo eyes blinking in a high ceilinged room that has been lit by candles and chandeliers; crossed and recrossed by merchants and gentry, butlers and servants from stairwell to pantry.

Max flicks a switch and the whole room plunges into darkness. Outside the window the fawning creatures with their fluttering fans and shuffling crepe dresses vanish in the blackness and only the gaunt silhouettes of cats remain, stalking and prowling round overfilled bins.

Max lights a cigarette and follows its glow across the room. Picks up his playlist and a clattering stack of CDs and plastic which he rattles into his carrier bag.

As he stands on the steps outside, slow cars drift through shadowy mist. The dim eyes of streetlamps watch the eyes which watch each other, sizing up their moves, languid as decay, sudden as disease.

Max slithers unnoticed between them, the ghost that no-one sees.

- 8 -

Max was in the room. They sensed his presence almost before they turned the radio on. As soon as they heard the riff, they knew. Without checking what station they were tuned in to.

That deep throat voice lurking the airwaves: *"Midnight Max coming to you. Block the dial. Unlock your eyes. Nobody sleeps from now till dawn."* A gravel growl to grab the spleen, churn the guts and chill the brain.

Power packed through a tiny radio. In the street outside a tall figure in a long drape raincoat stands and watches the block. Bedroom lights blink on and off. A jangle of TV soundtracks rattles a mix of screaming brakes, breaking screams, uncanned laughter and prepacked dreams.

Max's voice cuts through, continuing his litany. Luring the listeners away from the warmth, away from the light, out to embrace the depths of the night.

- 9 -

Under the bus-shelter she waits uneasily, feeling the eyes of the other women watching her. She turns away, pretending to scan the road again for the bus that never seems to come.

At the corner, sometime in the night, a hit-and-run has snapped the stem of the traffic lights, leaving them tilted back, angled to the sky, beaming out Amber, Stop and Go.

She tugs at the scarf knotted tight about her throat. To keep the rain off, but it's stopped now. Thin plastic mac hangs awkwardly, clinging to her legs.

One of the women coughs. Asks her point-blank if she knows the time, eyes drilling straight into hers and out the other side. But before she can say anything, someone else chimes in that it's nearly quarter-to.

And a car draws up. A man's voice, smiling like a knife. He holds the door open for her. She glances nervously at the watching women. The car would take her away from them. But the man, he's the last person she wants to see.

She shakes her head nervously, wondering what he'll say, but he just slams the door and drives away. The women nudge towards her. Then surge forward, but only to board the bus which has rumbled to a halt in front of them. The women crowd on, leaving her standing at the stop. As she tries to follow, the driver shakes his head.

"Full right up. There's another one behind."

And the doors hiss shut.

- 10 -

She shuffles aboard the bus, shaking away the last drops of rain that still cling to her as a reminder. Behind her sits a woman, ignoring the signs, choking a rosary of cigarette smoke, repeating a toneless litany over and over again.

"It's cold… and it's dark… so I don't want to go out… so I get on the bus… okay?...... OKAY."

The second OKAY defiant, emphatic, almost another voice answering the first, delivered after a pause during which unspoken responses well to the surface.

"It's cold… and it's dark… so I don't want to go out… so I get on the bus… okay?...... OKAY."

At the back a man with a flat cap pulled down tight on his head begins to sing like a broken jukebox of battered country hits. The passengers around him shuffle in their seats, move further forward, closer to the door.

They'd love to think he's just another drunk, but the voice is too firm, too true. If he was on stage or on TV, they'd burst into applause. But here on the bus, two seats away, he's too close for comfort, as each fragment of song floats seamlessly into the next and his eyes lock with theirs, a stare that insists, *"Listen to me. Listen to this."*

"It's cold… and it's dark… so I don't want to go out…"

At the next stop the man in the cap makes his way down the gangway, bowing and blowing kisses. He vaults lightly onto the pavement and the bus falls silent, but before anyone can vent their relief in pent-up laughter, they see him standing in the flickering limelight of the bus-shelter, still bowing and waving, but laughing at them.

At the back one half-hearted joker tries to pick up the song's last line and carry it on, but his voice hovers feebly, cracks and fades. Uneasily the passengers raise a smile, fall back to scrutinising the grimy darkness that weighs against the windows.

"... I don't want to go out... so I get on the bus... okay?...... OKAY."

- 11 -

Max staggers home, dizzy with words, with sounds, with silence.

Now the streets are empty with all the people who have not been listening to his voice on the radio. He never knows who they are. Sometimes they phone him. Sometimes hang up. A click, a self-satisfied purr. Sometimes ring in and beg to be connected with all the others who are listening and not listening. All the sleeping lovers and all the loving sleepers.

Beg to tell their story to anyone who'll listen. And in the end Max listens as the records turn. He lets the tapes roll, shuffling the sounds, dropping the playlist. Never bothering to stop and talk to the listeners who are listening while he listens to the listener who is talking.

Connection is everything. But in the empty street damp newspapers wrap round his ankles and tail-lights trail through the glistening mist. Dawn slips dull between beckoning streetlamps. Rooftops glower above him and sullen subways yawn.

An unseen hand clutches at his coat sleeve. Max stares back into the face that stares back at him. This is not someone who has sat alone listening to his show or drizzled out the dog-end of a party checking his sounds. Here is someone who has no radio. Has no telephone to dial in to tell him how lonely he is.

Connection is everything. This is someone who is not connected. Max shadow-dances the shadow one hazy moment. The voice in the throat clears to speak. But there are no words. No connection. No direction home.

- 12 -

She digs up the roses. She trawls their dark beds. She tears the wild marigolds off by their heads. She swears to the wind, to the trees, to the wall, that just like the man who planted them - she doesn't need them anymore.

But though her fingers are bloodied and torn by the snags of the thorns, she has no strength left to wrench out the roots which still cling in the soil and claw at the gall of her heart.

"The leaves leave the tree as my children leave me," she repeats as she beats at the path with a broom, watched by the house and its dark empty rooms.

As the sun slips away she gathers armfuls of petals, softer than flesh, spilling them in hithering thithering haste, a trail like a wedding; in the house and back again, in the house and back again, garnered into a heap in the middle of the sitting room floor.

The carpet's own pattern is a blaze of flowers and leaves - which she knows she's always hated. She only chose it because she knew that he would hate it more as he stumped in and out from the rose beds, muttering that it was unnatural to have flowers on a carpet, trapped between four walls. Flowers belonged in the garden, outside under the sun.

Now in the centre of the room she piles a dank mound of dull earth and twigs, thin branches and thorns; petals and leaves matted into the weave of the pattern beneath. As the cold room darkens and night's silence begins, the mirror above the empty hearth where no fire has burned for years catches the moon's reflection, a chiding sister, watching.

- 13 -

He slogs his way up the concrete stairs. Following the drip of the leaky mop bucket. He can tell when the Albie's been here before him.

Always the stairs. Never the lift. The lift's never working. Except.

Except as he climbs the stairs he always hears it whining past him. And voices inside laughing. If he does ever use the lift, nobody ever laughs. They all stare dumbly at the walls. Or wonder who owns the pair of mismatched shoes that rides in the corner beside them.

Slogs on up to the top. So he can make his way down again. Floor by floor. A slow helter skelter. Knocking on the doors.

"Rent."

He knocks again.

"Rent."

The door opens slowly, puzzled.

"What?"

"Rent."

"It's you."

"Yes - I know. That's right. It's me. Rent."

"But..."

"I know. But. You've had the letter. You have to take it down the Rent Office now. Or the Social's paying it direct. I'm not coming round anymore. The Rent Man. Too many muggings. It didn't say that. The letter. But that's what it meant."

"But..."

"But nobody ever mugged me. They all knew me. Knew half the time the bag was empty cos I let you all off too easy. No need to mug me when it's still in everyone's pockets. One more reason for the letter. No more rent men."

"But..."

But why am I here? I always come. Every week. Same day. Same time. The Rent Man. I always come. Up the stairs. Knock on the door. Say hello. See you're okay. What's different? Why change? Only the letter. No bag. No book. Only me. That's what I'd always say to the old ones. So as not to worry them. Only me. Forget the rent. Only me."

- 14 -

"Going far, stranger?"

He turns around. The sound of the voice is spiky, mean. Trails off into manic, high pitched laughter that stops suddenly. Dead. On the back seat sprawls a thin faced kid. Lizard eyes fixed. Fondles a knife between long fingers. One hand is bandaged, seeping blood.

There's only the two of them, up here on the top deck as the bus bounces its dream glide out through town. The neon fades as they hit the side roads, long avenues lit by sodium, muted and dull.

The man says nothing. What is there to say? He's not sure how far he's going anyway. Never been this route before.

The voice comes again, edged with sarcasm.

"I said - going far? Or didn't you hear?"

Graffiti on the seats. Anger and desperation. Lust and accusation. Exaggerated diagrams clamour for attention. Snakes tattooed all up the kid's arm. They writhe and twist and hiss to the knotting and unclenching of white-knuckle fists as a racking cough hacks out. A banshee wail. Unbroken pain.

The man rises to his feet, then sinks again, one hand still clinging uselessly to the bell cord that would connect him to the driver downstairs. But it does not ring. The bus rolls on, past the next empty stop.

The kid advances, knife outstretched. Eyes glinting dead metal.

The man recoils, judders for the cut. The kid reaches

inside the studded leather jacket draped across taut shoulders, still uttering the babbling scream. Rips open the front of a faded check shirt. One pale tit lets fall.

"Touch this, stranger," the gagging voice pleads. "Suck on this."

- 15 -

Had seen it all before. But it still hurts. Call this work? Called out after hours to board up space against the darkness. That unseen space that stands between what we expect - the easy warmth of sitting room, the seep of TV, chatter, cups of tea. And the outside. Biting wind, a spit of rain, the eyes of neighbours looking in, looking away, never knowing what to say, but saying plenty. Saying nothing.

She's in the corner of the room that is a room no more as the outside pours in. And the inside spills out.

I knock the shattered glass as careful as I can. Scoop it up into a pan. Tip it in the wheelie bin. But splintered glass gets everywhere; it's underfoot, it's in the air, it clings to hair, severs skin. Letting the inside out. Letting the outside in.

Poor girl. Only a girl. And she's got girlies too. And their nan just stands there, not knowing what to do; doing everything. Taking the little ones on her

knee. Making tea. She doesn't ask me. But I'm not here. I'm just boarding up the space. Against the dark. Against the night.

Against the man I've never met, who's brought me here to board the space to keep him out. Who put six bricks from the rockery he took so long to make

in the tiny garden with his own bare hands, with all his pride. Put six bricks through his own front window. To get back in. But not come in. Just to let the darkness through.

And the eyes of those who stand and stare. While one lad who saw it all, or says he did, tries to sell them knock-off tapes from underneath his coat.

Right underneath the busies' eyes. Who show no surprise. Just like me. Not even surprised not to get a cup of tea. Seen it all before. Call this work?

He's gone now, so they say. The man who lived here, who doesn't live here anymore. Shot away. Stopped him up the road when his car piled into the lights

on the corner. They said he just looked dazed. Like he didn't know what'd happened. Like he didn't know what he'd done. Just stood there staring at

the traffic signals tilted back. Amber, Stop and Go, angled into the sky from the top of their broken stem. Someone else's job to come fix them.

A morning job. Need the sun.

Seen it all before. Call this work?

- 16 -

"Screwy got done for robbing a car." Jacko listens as Degs tells him.

Jacko already knows, but if Degs tells him as well, it must be true. On the next bench the old guy unpacks his suitcase. A system of straps and strings. He keeps glancing around as if he's afraid someone will see him.

Jacko keeps watching him as he listens to Degs, but the old guy doesn't seem to mind, as if Jacko doesn't count.

"He wired it out the Kwickie car park. Got it round to their block. Sparks everywhere. Then he saw the busies creeping up behind him so he ditched the car and made off on this BMX he grabbed from outside theirs. The busies went after him but he wouldn't stop, so they swerved across in front of him down by the lights and knocked him off the bike."

The old guy pulls a bundle of newspaper out of the suitcase. Unwraps it slowly. There's sandwiches inside. A starling hops up. Then another. Squawking at the sparrows to drive them away.

"Screwy was hurt. Not bad, like. Winded and cuts and bruises. The busies grabbed him and hauled him round to his house. They knocked on the door and Screwy's old man answers it and they says, 'Is this your lad?' - as if they didn't know."

The old guy tears a corner off one of the sandwiches. Scatters it in the middle of the pack of pecking birds. Jacko can just about see that what spills out as filling is not meat or lettuce or cheese. It's newspaper. Bits of old newspaper. The birds peck at it disappointed, scavage the bread, then flap away.

"Screwy's old man starts giving them loads of verbal for knocking Screwy down. Then Screwy's knees just give on him and he sort of keels over. Delayed shock, like. The busies bundle him inside and stick him on the sofa.

"While one of them's talking to his dad, telling him about Screwy and the motor, the other's nosing round the flat..."

"...and it's stashed with all kinds of videos and robbed tellies," Jacko says.

"So that's how come Screwy's dad got done as well..." Degs trails off, watching Jacko's face as he watches the old guy slowly chomping away at his newspaper sandwiches.

- 17 -

He sits on his suitcase in the middle of the mud-filled park. Watches the woman who crosses the grass. Crosses and recrosses as if she is weaving a pattern, dancing a dance. In her hands there are flowers the colour of faded summers. She has picked them from the beds of the park where they wither among flapping carrier bags, broken bottles and twisted bicycle frames.

But she doesn't just pick them, she scatters them too. As if they are part of the pattern. As if she gives one to each of her partners in this invisible waltz.

The old man beats a drumbeat on the side of his case. A weathered smile spreads across his face. This woman could be his sister, dancing on the beach. Running, calling, hiding - then skittering out of reach.

The gulls still swoop above, just as they always did. Gather and glide as his sister runs, as the woman runs, awkwardly, dropping the flowers as he lurches towards her, calling her name. Calling his sister's name. Calling.

And sinking defeated to the beat of the drum as he flails at his suitcase. The rhythm of the sea.

- 18 -

A magpie hops, head cocked to one side, towards the bench in the windblown park where Jacko sits down with the old man.

"*One for sorrow. Two for joy.* That's the song we used to sing when we saw magpies sitting in a tree. But what do you think the magpies say when they see you and me?"

Jacko shrugs. The bird struts inquisitively, then suddenly flaps away.

The old man counts on his fingers.

"*One for sorrow... Two for sorrow...*"

Jacko shuffles, not sure why he's here now, sitting next to this dishevelled stranger who smells of garlic and rain.

The old man coughs. "It is the rhythm of the sea," he says. "The rhythm of the sea draws us from our beds. The rhythm of the sea turns the thunder in our heads. The rhythm of the sea sucks the moon like a frightened egg."

He unbuckles the strap that fastens his battered suitcase. Inside there is a blanket, the colour of twilight, the shadow of dust. He shakes it out. Underneath lies a cluster of packages, wrapped in old newspaper and plastic bags. Fastened with ribbon and bits of twisted string.

"Open one," the old man says.

Jacko struggles nervously, fingers picking at the slippery knots. Finally peels back the wrapper of yellowing headlines. Inside there is a mirror. Cracked and misted with a film of grease, it still refracts the sad grey sky that hangs above them, and one gawky magpie, circling.

"How many birthdays do you have, son?"

"One," Jacko mutters, puzzled.

"Give the mirror back," the man demands suddenly.

Jacko hands it to him.

"No, not like that. Wrap it up. Wrap it up," the man explains.

Jacko bunches the paper hurriedly to cover the fragment of sky. Fumbles the cats-cradle of string. The old man sits patiently till the parcel's handed back to him.

"How many birthdays do *I* have, son?"

"I don't know." Jacko senses there must be some trick.

"Well, you won't know till you ask me. Go on. Ask me. Go on."

"How many birthdays...?"

"Every day," the old man says. "Every days's my birthday. All the parcels - I've got them here. I can give myself a present every day of the year."

A second magpie lands.

- 19 -

Each day they share the stairs, the same front door, but nothing more. Their lives do not connect. Except here. Each day before him in the bathroom she dabs her freshly lip-sticked lips and discards the tissue paper kiss into the toilet bowl. There it floats, a breath on the water.

Max comes in after. And takes delight in aiming straight between the lips he's never kissed. That have never touched him. He never can be sure whose lips they are. She has always gone through the shared front door, out into the sun, before he can ever know for sure who she is, which one.

In the hallway the house smells of cat crap. Shadows haunt the litter of left over junk that has been here for years. A bicycle wheel, a map of a battle, a faded print of a painting entitled 'Eventide' that portrays two anguished lovers, locked in a desperate embrace. Two mismatched shoes. Everything nobody wants, but nobody wants to throw away.

Max puzzles sometimes over the cat crap. He never knows which cats live here, who they belong to, who feeds them. And doesn't care. The musky smell drifts up the stairs. And the people come and go like cats themselves, slinking stealthily, in and out the front door just like another cat flap. Carrying their silence with them as they go. A silence which fills each room, seeps into the dust of the landings.

Sometimes mingled with the silence, there will be the sound of crying, a muffled argument, an echo of loving. But all so muted, so breathless, as if from another house, another time. The ghosts of the rooms.

Max flushes the toilet. Checks his hair. Makes his way slowly down the stairs. This morning on the square of faded linoleum where the front door mat used to be, a second tissue lies, its lipstick trace fainter than the first. Like a whisper. An unexpected letter. Sealed With A Loving Kiss.

- 20 -

Catseye glasses slither down her nose as she trudges up the stairs of the block. A can of paint juggled in each hand. Each can dribbles and drips its colour behind her. A trail to nowhere. At each landing she stops and changes hands, reversing the colour code.

A majorette's stick stuck under her arm. It clatters across the concrete steps each time she drops it, her hands growing numb as she sets down the cans to pick it up, leaving two rings of ghostly colour imprinted on the stair.

Staring at the numbers, checking them off as she continues her climb to the top. Following her own trail of the day before, the week before, as she's humped trip after trip of paint to her door.

Her door is ratcheted with locks. Mortice, yale and padlock riven into the split and rotting timber of the shaky frame and the purple painted plywood, fortressed against the concrete. Shutting out the sky, here at the top of the world. A cat's cradle of metal. Setting down the cans again she jangles a handful of keys from the bunch that rattles round her waist. She is her own jailor and sets herself free from the prison of the world into the sweet release of her cell. Cracks the door behind her, snapping the bolts and shackling the chains.

The passage is a litter of newspapers spread across the floor to catch the shreds of wallpaper she's been peeling from the wall. Scraping and shredding and cursing and fussing. Layer after layer. Great overblown flowers, gaudy and garish, zigzag patterns and squint-eyed swirls. Each layer pasted up by each of the tenants who were here before. Who lived up here on the fourteenth floor.

Even posters and press-cuttings papered between the paper, a papier-mâché history book that she strips away, chipping and nibbling day by day.

Setting the cans down again, she levers open the sitting room door. A rainbow of colours writhes across the wall, her own contribution to the flat's mosaic of history. Half-open paint pots strewn about the floor. Nothing else in the room. No carpet, no TV, no furniture at all except one sagging sofa that was here when she came, that leaks mysterious photographs and letters without names.

The rainbow frames the window where she settles now to view the opposite block like a grey lump of rock melting in the rain. But half-way down its cliff-face, lit bright as an eye which cannot see her - though she can peer right into it - is the room where Skin plays his guitar. She cannot hear him, but watches him play. Night after night. Day after day.

- 21 -

Today on her birthday she places the cards on the dresser again. The ones she keeps from year to year. No-one sends her cards anymore. Unless she remembers to put them in envelopes and take them to the post. And wait for them to come back next day, rattling through the letter box.

But sometimes some of them go astray. They come a day late, or folded or crushed. Or delivered to someone else streets away, who won't know why they've come, what they're for.

She's bought a cake. With icing, with cream. With a candle on the top. But no name. Just plain. She wonders whether to eat it now. Or wait to see who comes. But no-one will come. She knows that. Though she's set the places just incase.

No-one will come to this house, where she lives with people she never sees. Where the dust never changes in the hall and she stumbles past the bicycle wheel to get to the door: the two mismatched shoes, the map of a battle, the two longing lovers trapped in a frame.

"But I don't want to go out... it's cold... and it's dark... I don't want to go out... the sky's full of rain... I can feel it in my head... in a cloud shaped like pain..."

She closes the door again. Back in the room she pats her hair. Applies fresh lipstick to the blood-red smear. Touches her mouth with a tissue which drifts towards the bin. But doesn't go in.

She rearranges her birthday cards. Tall ones at the back, the small ones at the front. Mouths the verses, the greetings. Many Happy Returns. It returns again and again. She wonders where's the happiness.

Wears her birthday dress. Clowns a clumsy curtsey. Curses as ash spills down it from another cigarette.

"I don't want to go out... so I get on the bus... okay?...... OKAY."

The second OKAY defiant, emphatic, almost another voice answering the first, delivered after a pause during which she resolutely takes one card and turns its face to the wall.

In the hall the letterbox rattles. There's a clatter of feet on the stairs. But when she reaches the landing there's no envelopes on the floor. Nobody's there.

"OKAY."

- 22 -

Rafferty travels between zones. Invisible barriers that freeze each street. Only graffiti and birdsong know where are the boundaries. Knots of kids cruising the kerbways. Old grandmothers standing in doorways. On the corner-shops the shutters are locked. Above street level where nobody looks, rust-etched signs proclaim *Players Please, Hovis* and *Lux*. Thistledown drifts the wasteland. Whispering connections.

The flowers smell of passion. Of dust. Of dirt. Of hurt that floods a siren's dirge up from the bloodshot river. She mixed bad medicine and no-one would forgive her.

He drives the van through streets where daughters dream they're mothers pushing too-big baby buggies; and mothers dream they're daughters again, out on the town in their finery with no-one but themselves to come home to. All the clocks have stopped as silent walls lean sideways in a soporific haze where the suddenly old sit with the suddenly young to watch the sunset's slow parade.

Rafferty hashes his options, snarling at the lights. Crumbling tenements to the left, boarded shop fronts turning right. White van meshing, speeding across town, flitting unseen between half-light and neon. Payload on the dashboard. Wheels grinding round. Spinning and deceiving. Delivering and receiving.

He guns past the 66 bus, heading out along tree-lined avenues. Gardens choked with loneliness as sunset hangs in the air. From faceless curtained windows, rooms of silence stare.

She watches the street with eyes too tired for hunger. Tracking the days, a gaze gaunt with languor. Waiting for the engine's deep-throat roar, more urgent than any lover.

Her feet almost fall down the stairs, so anxious to open the door. Rafferty stands in the driveway, his white van coated in a cloak of dust, parked out on the roadway, the other side of the wrought-iron gates.

"I've been waiting," she says, as packages exchange hands.

Rafferty says nothing, he never does. She closes the door before he's even through the gate. Shutting out the coming twilight, the blackbird's fading serenade, the lingering scent of the flowers.

Rafferty climbs into the van. Ratchets the gears. Drives across town.

- 23 -

She's dancing now. Giving it the boogaloo, the shakedown shuffle. Move those hips. Shake those tits. Arse as wide as the back end of a bus that rides route 66.

"69. Eyes down for a line." After the bingo the band come on. And she comes on. To the band. Everytime.

The minute the music starts she's up on her feet. Manoeuvring her girth skilfully round the dance floor. If the band's never played this club before they just don't know what they've got coming. And nobody ever lets on. By the second number she's up on stage, egging the singer to bump and grind. They never know whether to leave her to it or carry on with the song. Sometimes they hand her the microphone and walk away. But it's okay. She knows she can't sing. She only wants a chance to dance.

And she can. The same routine, week out, week in. Disco bop and belly flop. She means no harm. Grabs the spindly singer and spins him like a mop. He leans in closer and whispers in her ear. Her face looks shocked.

"There's no need for that, lad. All's I'm after is a bit of fun."

They give her a round of applause anyway, as she shadow-waltzes back to her place, and the band rock on, wondering why they've come, wondering why they bother. The singer grins sheepishly and hopes she's not brought her brother.

- 24 -

The bottom of the pan is burnt. Sticky memories scraped across its surface. A long last supper staring breakfast in the face. This is my body. This is my blood. Do this in....

Her fingers touch congealed grease. Soft as flesh. This my body. But cold. No life on these bones that she rattles into the bin. Take, drink. Is this a sin? That we consume each other so. What do we take? What is taken? What do we leave? What is there left?

Her fingers touch her own body. But not in the way. That he could touch her. That he would.

She feels the blood. Plates streaked and stained, a web of pain.

Outside the garden is growing. She feels it grow. Like juice between her fingers. One hand wants to hack, to chop, to cut. The other wants to stroke, to soothe, to peel. To heal this ache which wells inside her.

Outside the birds are singing. The fluting mawk as they wheel and turn, learning a world which is tiny and vast.

She watches the sky through one square of window. Trapped and free. Trapped and free. Opens one shutter and listens. Beyond the birds, beyond the sunset, beyond the city's numb roar of traffic. She listens for one sound. Pulsing across the map of her body. One sound, one engine, one long white van which will stand at the end of the driveway. And the knock on the door.

He will come.

She kisses her fingers, sweet as the shadows which fill this room, fill her body, lift her limbs, swim soft and gentle inside her head.

Outside the flowers smell of passion. Of dust. Of dirt. Of hurt that floods a siren's dirge up from the bloodshot river. She mixed bad medicine and

no-one would forgive her.

But now she waits for the knocking. Soon he will come. Soon as the night. Soon as darkness. Across the city's slow traffic of dreams.

He will come.

- 25 -

She lights another cigarette. Lets it smoke. Lets it bleed. Watches as ash spills pale and grey all down her pleated birthday dress.

Outside the sky is full of rain. She can feel it in her head, in a cloud shaped like pain. She goes down to the hall again. Tries the light switch. It doesn't work. It never does. Peering through the gloom she makes out the print of a painting of two sweethearts captured forever in desperate embrace.

She hugs herself. She would like to. Like to be like that woman. Someone to hold her. Anyone would do. Just to be held. But she looks again. The eyes echo pain, like the pain in her head. Maybe he holds her too tightly. Maybe he won't let her go.

She wonders what his name is. Tries to make out the letters just above the frame. Slowly spells out "Eve...". But that man isn't Adam, and that garden's never Eden.

Smudges red lips with the back of her sleeve. Back in her room the cards that she placed on her dresser have all fallen down on the floor. She bends to pick them up again, repeating the names that are written inside. Tracing the words with her fingers.

Except that name. She won't say that name ever again. But she still keeps the card and wonders why. Sends it off each year with the others. Addressed to herself. So they can all come back to stand on the shelf. Sometimes they go, and never come back. Maybe she wrote her own name wrong, or the post couldn't read the address. But that one, with that name. Always comes back. Always comes back first.

She seems to fall asleep, then wakes again. It's later now. Nobody came. The cake is untouched, with the candle, the cream. She lights another cigarette.

Turns the radio on. It's nearly midnight. Nearly time. Soon the day will be over. She can put the cards back for another year. But now she can listen to that voice. The one which talks to her. She feels chill fingers touch her spine as she hears him open up the line.

"Block the dial. Unlock your eyes. Nobody sleeps from now till dawn."

Not at all. Sometimes she thinks she never sleeps now. Not at all. Not in that bed she never gets into. No way of knowing who's slept there before. Each night listening to that voice. That voice which haunts like a waking dream. Which stems the scream that is rising inside her.

But she knows she sleeps sometimes in the day. In the chair. Though she wouldn't say. The hours just seem to slip away.

"For all you lonely lovers and all you loving loners, this is where you get connected. Just pick up the phone..."

She does. Just this once. She never has before. But it's her birthday. Well it was. She never has before. Not made the connection. She's dialled often enough. Dialled and hung up. Never got through. But tonight she is there. His voice talking to her voice, filling the air. Except she can't make the words. Can think of no words to say, out of all the words that she wanted to say.

"Is there somebody there? Talk to me. Talk..."

His words confuse her, coming down the phone line, tumbling from the radio, filling the room. She feels herself crying, though she knows she doesn't want to. She does. She silently sobs, hot tears welling in the mouthpiece of the phone.

"Is there somebody there?" she asks in the end, repeating his question, as the voice on the radio falls silent.

The words spill back as she says them, out of the radio, into the room where they came from. Then nothing, just silence turning round, building into a howl of electric sound.

"Talk to me..."

She pleads with the silence.

"Talk..."

- 26 -

Skin climbs onto the 66 bus. A haze of faces blurs his stare. He heads straight towards the only empty seat. Perches on the edge. The seat is broken, sagging in the middle. He looks down onto the floor. Beside him are two mismatched shoes. His nose wrinkles. He's aware of an acrid smell, like the shadow of dead rain. Skin leans forward, trying to escape the smell, scanning the back pages of other passengers' newspapers. He looks around, about to move, but there are no more empty seats on the bus.

Out the window he sees the man who sits everyday at the crossroads, grinning like a child, waving a ragged handful of flowers at the bus. No-one waves back.

It's like sitting on a plank, this seat. From the back a kid in studded leather smothered in snake tattoos thrusts down the gangway, lizard eyes fixed. The bus brakes squeal as if in pain, easing to halt at the side of the road. The kid jumps off. Skin moves back to claim the empty space, leaving the broken seat with its two ghost shoes and lingering smell.

At the next stop, by the park, a woman boards. She clutches a bunch of flowers, but the stems are snapped, the heads bent and broken, showering petals. She stares distractedly through the window, seeing nothing, seeing something no-one else can see. But not seeing that the seat is broken. Not seeing the two mismatched shoes. Not smelling that lingering, personal smell. Or not caring.

There's a sticky sweet wedged under the window. It

clings to her coat. She scrapes it free and licks her fingers. Wipes them slowly down her skirt. Sits upright, suddenly gazing at the flowers in her hand, wondering why she might have them. Her other hand tests the seat. She stands up hastily, feet kicking the shoes as she looks around, lighting on another space next to Skin.

She sits down beside him, not sure what to say. Not sure what to do with the flowers. For a moment she seems about to present them to Skin, then stops herself, realising he wouldn't know why, or what to do.

Skin turns his gaze out into the street and catches sight of a figure at a window. He's seen her so often before. Never in the garden, always at the window. She seems to be watching, just seems to wait.

The brakes wail as the bus stops again and another woman climbs on, juggling two pots of paint, her cats-eye glasses sliding down her nose as she drops a majorette's stick, picks it up again. Sits down in the only empty seat.

As the sweet sticks in turn to her coat, two lads behind her start to giggle. The other passengers just stare blankly. No-one says anything. But she stays where she is, not noticing the shoes, or even their smell, as both of her cans start to dribble a puzzle of paint on the floor. The doors open and close, seats become vacant, but she doesn't move, just sits there, breathing heavily onto the window and doodling strange dancing figures all over the glass as her paint cans rattle and drip on the floor.

- 27 -

He crawls from under fallen rubble.

In the shimmering heat his skin changes. Changes shape, changes colour. Textures shift. Until.

He is grey. He is assembled. He is charged.

Beyond him stretches an alienscape. Structures and towers. Tracts of random wasteground. Desolation flowering beside gardens of creatures who move and glow, dance and hesitate, dream and glide. He looks into their eyes for a sign, but their language tumbles, stuttering and ugly from a cavity torn in the front of their face. Desperate sounds, fractured and snarling, lilting and guarded.

They carry their bodies upright as if they trust no-one, always looking around. Looking for sounds. He does not understand. How to see.

Their sex glands are covered as if they are ugly, as if they are dangerous.

A love letter is scrawled on a wall. The sounds have been fixed into shapes. But it makes no sense, it makes no sense. There are no signs in the eyes. There are no eyes in the walls.

The creatures move towards him as if not seeing him at all. And yet they acknowledge he is there as they move round him, move past him. To avoid. No signs in their eyes. No recognition at all.

Until one who is smaller than the rest makes a noise like fear which flows. But the torn hole in the face twists upward. Like a friend who wants to be an enemy. Like an enemy who wants to be a friend.

And there's a flicker of sign in the eyes. To say *you are here and I am too.*

Perhaps the small one is also strange to the others. He holds out a hand. Tries to shape the gurgling sound any way that he can.

But then there are more. More small ones. From behind the stacks of metallic bricks. From behind the sheets of silver which reflect the sun more brightly than it ever should. Which hurt his eyes. He covers them. As he covers them the gurgling sound comes.

Happy.

This is happy. And friend.

He holds out hands again. But the gurgling grows louder and they strike him with fragments of ragged wood. Sharp pebbles hit his flesh. He feels the skin changing, resisting. Feels a sensation which registers pain. Though that will not translate. It is a hurt which he does not understand.

It does not translate.

There is no sign.

- 28 -

Salt. It was the salt he wanted. That salt to be found in the soft places, the sweet places, bathing the texture of glistening skin, caressed by the subtle singing of darkness.

Brought forth by the touching, the mouthing, the movement, the stillness. In every membrane and tendon, the juices, the pleasure.

He could feel that these creatures craved it too. Smell it in the wind. Sign it in their eyes. And yet they always turned away, denied it, suppressing their craving until it became sickness.

It was the smell of salt that he followed, licking at eyelids, all the gathering places, crevices, tracing between the shadows of bricks, the caverns of steel, wanting to release all the feelings.

Wanting to taste the salt which coursed freely from bloodstream to brain cell to nerve-end to knowledge to wonder to life.

But they turned away. Turned away from him. Turned away from each other and turned their hunger their longing their loving on themselves.

Leaving just shadows.

Licking their wounds.

- 29 -

Oil.

Is the balm. Is the calming. Is the glide. Is anointment of body of touch of skin. Of flesh. Sweet flesh. And inside.

Where world cannot touch but all world is there. To taste to scent to relish and explore.

There is always more.

The slipping, the sliding to rivulet and cavern and well source. Flesh enters flesh as soft as breathing as soft as caress.

Yes the breathing is tender is liquid. It sighs and it whispers. The rhythm of oceans. Travelling without time.

In this caress we move distances. The universe is open is endless is relentless. Is alive inside every one of us. To touch to open to drive.

And oil.

Salt and oil. Flesh and kiss. This is the journey. Eons and ages. One touch away.

Cavities and craters. Mountains and volcanoes, dark steaming forests. Lost deep within us.

- 30 -

Beneath the coat, his skin transmutes. Rainbow to grey. They would understand a neutral shade. He hopes. Colour of cloud. Colour of smoke.

Here on this park bench he sits. Small ones all around. He has learnt to avoid them. Learnt to ignore them. But still he must watch, must learn.

Now again they surround him. Bind him in a web of high-pitched sound. But their eyes sign. They are happy. What do they call him?

Clown.

He shrugs and watches as they walk bent and floppy. Trip on something he cannot see. And fall down.

He feels moved to copy. As he stands he feels his skin shuffling through a skein of glowing colours. Beyond his control.

The small ones watch, sat in a circle. Watch him clumsily follow the movements, the rag doll walk, the stumbling fall.

He stops. That is all he knows, all that they showed him. They bang their hands together, a fractured sound, like a flock of startled birds.

One magpie watches them, head on one side. Joined by another. Joy for two.

He adjusts his coat. Flips a sudden backflip. A handstand, a cartwheel. Not clumsy now. Moving in shapes and patterns the small ones have never seen before. A blur of movement, of colour, of light. The coat slips away as he whirls, a dervish of energy.

The small ones bang their hands again. Their voices shriek with the pain of pleasure. They rock and tumble. Clamour for more.

He stops. They are being watched. From another bench an old one, stooping, pretending not to see what he can see. Busies himself with a box which he carries by a handle of twisted string. The whole box is swathed in a cradle of string. The old one begins to unpick it, still watching. Unwraps a parcel of grimed printed paper.

One of the magpies hops up to his feet.

The old one laughs. Not like a clown. Like a cracked ringmaster. Like a circus crowd snarling with fear.

The small ones look over, look away as he begins to beat the case like a drum. On and on. As if commanding the show to begin. Scaring away the ring of birds. Scaring away the ring. Scaring...

But when the small ones turn back to their own clown, for comfort, for reassurance, they discover he has gone.

- 31 -

A trapped kite flaps against the telegraph wires, sullen grey wind tugging at its tailstrings. It hangs bedraggled between the houses, an exotic dream-bird lost in this chasm of breezeblock and concrete. It remembers flight, remembers the sweet height of sun over hills, the shrill pulse of singing, ringing the clouds. But then it falls back, checked by the wire that snags at its own wire, an anchor which aches with every breath, every movement.

The rain has stopped as the faded plastic struggles to fly, ripped by long gashes of glass and flung stones.

A seagull spreads its wings as wide as the street, then lands, clattering and cawping, its harsh throated voice brine rusted and ghost racked, stepping over a picture of a glistening river ripped from a glossy magazine which floats slowly towards the scudding gutter across the still-drenched pavement.

The kite flaps again. From the distant railway line a desolate whistle wails.

- 32 -

In a half-lit cafe at the end of a derelict street, a girl is dancing on a small raised stage.

The cafe is empty. The tables heavy with dust and silence. Shadows come and go, to sit hunched over one cup of coffee, a slow cigarette. Pages from old newspapers slither to the floor.

The girl dances on, her hair tied back in a dun-coloured scarf, her pleated skirt swaying casually. She dances as if she is waiting for a lover she has never met, but no-one ever comes.

The occasional customers take no notice of her. The pot-bellied man behind the bar continues as if she is not there at all. He mops the floor and wipes the top of the counter, but always the dust returns, spinning in the spectral light beside the curtained stage.

He runs a hand across his balding head and rubs his greasy hair. Tugs at his braces and starts to whistle.

As he whistles he gazes across at the stage. The girl is dancing faster now, her pale lips twisting into a smile.

The man busies himself, polishing glasses, stacking plates, emptying tarnished ashtrays into the depths of a grimy bin.

He whistles faster as he works and the girl dances quicker too, clapping her hands and clicking her heels in a flurry of rhythm.

The man locks and bolts the door, closes the blinds. He has stopped whistling now. He takes a broom and slowly sweeps the empty stage.

There is no-one there at all.

- 33 -

In a deserted doorway, an uncontrolled shuffle. He does not dance for money. He does not dance for mirth. His face is set like a mask of stone, staring dreadful at the watching sun which watches him when no-one else will. They shuffle past, dwarfed by advertising hoardings, high brick walls, towering chimneys. They do not dance, they cannot.

Between two bin bags a pile of rags shifts. It is a figure, wrapped in a long grey coat. He squats on haunches, watching the dancer. His head moves rhythmic, side to side. His hands and feet beat out the measure, slapping damp paving stones to a melody no-one can hear, not even the dancer who continues his lone display, gazing unnerving direct at the sun.

The figure shrugs and shuffles closer, tugging the overcoat's folds round his shoulders. He signs to the dancer. But no reply. He takes the space on the pavement before him, mimicking the movements danced in the doorway. The dancer continues his own gyrations, a machine out of time, puppet robot. Until suddenly he just walks away, not dancing now, a straight line march, mingling in with the others who do not dance, disappearing down the street.

The figure takes his place in the doorway. Begins the dance, his overcoat flowing in time to the music which nobody can hear but which pours from the tower blocks, the windows, the eyes of passersby, though they cannot feel as it flows in colours, in waves of energy through the air.

- 34 -

As he pushed the door open he thought he could sense her presence in the room. A weight of warm air. That odour, the sweetness of leaves, catching at the back of his throat.

He could almost hear her voice, but her voice was not there, just its traces, spinning lightly as a texture of fingerprints across dust, touching here, touching there. Touching as her body would brush against him, sensual as sunlight, delighting in the accidents of contact, her cascading laughter hardly trying to deny that every caress was calculated.

But though the voice had its echoes in distant birdsong and the rustle of leaves through the open window, it was not there. Though it ached inside him, mouthing unspoken words, until his own thoughts merged with hers.

As he crossed the room, he noticed on the desk a scatter of opened books, as if she had been reading. And a letter, half written. He puzzled over the words, the characters. Their shapes seemed to shift as he attempted to focus them, as if they were written in a language he did not understand, did not even recognise.

Beyond the desk, the window half open. A rhapsody of evening light, distant voices calling. And the boughs of the trees moving rhythmically, making a music to which a shadow danced languidly across the velvet grass.

It was her. She danced with a vibrant energy as if she were not alone. As if she held a partner and their movements shared one pulse, as if they knew where to touch each other, where to hold, to caress, to move, to produce a rapture of pleasure.

Her eyes were closed. Her lips were open. Her fingers stroked shadows. And yet there was no-one there. From her throat let loose a whispering moan, lost in the music of the trees.

From the gathering darkness of the room he watched, then almost without thinking, picked up the unfinished letter from the desk as he retreated towards the door.

- 35 -

It's nearly Christmas. Rafferty is flogging Easter Eggs. Next year's, last year's, nobody knows. Blowing on cold fingers as he stands at the tailgate of his van, colour of dull slush, keeling into the mud.

"Get your eggs. Going cheap. Selling like hot cakes, misses. Two for a pound. Three for a quid."

"I'll take two."

"Thankyou." Rafferty squints sideways. Someone's standing watching him. Knots of customers grout and grume around the makeshift steaming stalls on this back end, back street market.

Rafferty shrugs, slippery silver slithering into his pockets.

At the next stall stands a man with a scar slash down his face like a chain from ear to chin. He does not speak. The clutches of shoppers follow his finger to see where he's pointing, to see what he sees. But everywhere he points there is emptiness. Nothing to see except cold droplets of fog. But still he mouths soundless words at the void.

A man in a duffle coat is standing close beside him, gripping packages of shopping. One parcel drops. He bends to pick it up, then straightens, and as he does his hood slips back to show that his face is scarred too.

Suddenly the first man speaks to him, the first words he's made all day, as if their wounds might bind them, comrades, brothers, warriors. But the words have no shape, drift lost into the emptiness, and the man in the duffle coat gathers his parcels and walks away.

"Three for a quid? You're alright - I'll take the two."

"...Thank*you*... Yes luv, they're just what you want. Christmas Eggs. Easter Pies. I got them all. All one size...."

"I don't know why I'm telling you this but everything's a mess. There's dirty washing in the sink and the dog's gone missing and Rafferty's done one of his vanishing tricks, been gone for days in that van. And I'm so sick with it I'm happy and I'm so happy with it I'm sick and I don't want him back and I wish he'd come home, if only for the sake of the dog. It would be up all night whining for him if it was here. But it's not.

"Maybe if he came home the dog would too and I hate them both. Hate their mess. There's dirty washing in the sink and my head's splitting and everything's a mess and I'm sorry, I don't know why I'm telling you this…"

On a low hung telephone wire the silhouettes of two dark birds peck and scrabble, preen and strut, above the two women in the street below.

"Donna, don't fuss yourself. You know it's alright. You know that you know where he is. You know Rafferty never goes far. To tell you the truth I'm sick of the sight of him myself. You know how it is."

A wall-eyed cat plays catch and chase with an empty can. Watching the birds as they watch him. None of them really watching the can.

"…I know, I know. First night home he can't do enough. He's all over you everywhere with his smiles and his eyes."

"…And then next morning he's under that van, tinkering and prodding with his hands full of oil. So you wouldn't want him touching you even if you wanted him to."

The can rattles and clatters, spilling a trail of ripe red juice. Spreading like sunset in an oil stained puddle.

"So he's with you, Donna?"

"Sure, Donna, same as ever."

On the wire the birds squawk loudly as they swap places, swap sides, exchange territories while the cat slinks low on its belly, no longer knowing which one is which.

"Just wondered, just wanted to be sure. It's really the dog that's getting to me. Can't stand it myself but Rafferty thinks the world of it and I wouldn't want him to come home and find that it was gone."

"Dogs. Don't you hate them?"

"Never trust them."

"Same as men."

The wheel of a white car crushes the can as it mounts the side, radio blaring with the window open wide.

"How's your Carla?"

"How's your Lee?"

"Same as ever."

"Can't complain."

From the distant railway line a desolate whistle wails. On the wire a trapped kite is flapping. The cat slinks away. Both of the birds have gone.

- 37 -

He straightens up and realises, as if for the first time, that a blackbird has been singing, accompanying his work. He rests his weight on the handle of the spade, ready to listen, to spend a few moments absorbed in its song. But the blackbird freezes, unsure of its audience, and rises to the rooftop, watching the man in the square of his garden, hedged in by privet fence, trellis and wall.

The dark earth is raked and tidy now, almost like a carpet. She'd like that he muses, placing the spade back in its space in the rack in the shed, the regimented row of glowering tools. Season to season the ritual rotation of digging of planting of compost of seed. Of lifting and tugging, of weeding and bedding. Of long hours spent in that potting shed, plotting and planning.

He stomps his feet by the door. Not one grain of earth to enter the kitchen, to defile the sheen of the spotless tiled floor, the ranks of bright saucepans anxiously gleaming, the line of best china on the shelf on the wall.

He strays into the sitting room, the carpet a blaze of flowers and leaves. Unnatural, he calls it, unneeded. Flowers belong in the garden, to flourish, to blossom, to gladden. Not woven into a carpet where their overblown colours collide with the wallpaper, clash with the shrill of the television which sits like an unloved child in the corner, imprisoning them all. Real flowers should wither, should shrivel, should die, should moulder and mulch till they rise again proud, reborn in the spring.

His arm knocks the ashtray and he bends to retrieve it, placing it exactly in its allotted position. On a mantelpiece packed with an array of ornaments, baubles and trinkets, the clock ticks relentlessly, summoning the darkness in the sullen mirror which watches him from above the empty hearth.

Again he realises the blackbird is singing, not in the garden, but high on the roof. He pauses by the settee, straightening the cushions, aware not so much of the blackbird outside, but of the silence inside, seeping through each fastidious room. Just now, at an hour when her presence would be filling the house, with poking and preening, polishing and cleaning, she has gone.

- 38 -

Far below, beneath the wheeling, screeching gulls, the small boy stands, peering over the bottom railing of the balustrade at the sandcastles and candyfloss which seem just out of reach as he gazes longingly down to the beach, tugging at the hand which holds him, soft and gentle, firm and strong.

He grips the rail stubbornly. He sees the big waves, coming, coming. It is the rhythm of the sea. But from the beach he hears a beat, a drum which comes from nowhere, somewhere. Nowhere he can see.

It comes from a crab-eyed, candy-striped tent, red and orange, orange and red, hanging between the sand and the sun. And a voice which shouts, which calls him. Which makes him want to run. He tugs at the hand which holds him, which draws him the other way, till reluctantly she follows him, leads him, down the concrete ramp, crusted with salt and shingle, which takes them to the beach. The sand is hot, it burns his feet as it ripples between his toes.

The drumbeat stops and he stands and gawps at the knockabout puppets which cannot talk, which squeal and bleat a story he cannot understand, as he holds her hand.

As he loosens her hand. When the puppets have gone and his eyes brim with tears. He wants to know who has taken them, why they're not here as he runs to the back of the candy-striped tent and jerks the curtain aside.

To find a man in an old raincoat bending over a

battered suitcase as he packs them away, the Judy, the Punch, the crocodile; who smiles as he pulls the suitcase shut and binds it with a cats-cradle of string. Then rises suddenly, lurching at the boy, with garlic breath and unwashed tongue.

And as he runs, he hears the beat of that distant drum.

And the woman running after him, reaching out her clutching hand. Calling till he giggles giddily, chasing between the gawping figures.

Till he lets her catch him and suddenly safe they run on and on, out onto the firm wet sand towards the crash of the calling sea.

Where he sees his sister, who has been waiting, playing and waiting, out by the rock pools and the anemones. She smiles when she sees them, and runs and laughs, towards them and away.

Away across the endless sand where the gulls swoop above, gather and glide as she runs. In her hand something glints like a mirror in the sun, a secret of silver which glimmers far beyond him. And because she has it, that's why he wants it as she tantalises, teases, as she runs, calling, hiding - then skittering out of reach as she leads him a dance the length of the beach. And he calls her name, again and again, lurching towards her. Falling.

As in the distance, from the candy-striped tent with its suitcase of mysteries, the drum beats on and on.

- 39 -

Ghost dreams. Unreal as loving. Losing colours. Awake in a sleeping room. Murmuring voices caress the silence. Hung moon waiting in the mirror's frame. Emptiness watches outside the window, whispering her name.

Trix shakes the dice. Her number's up. Whatever happens next, the dice are always right. Their numbers are messages, signals, codes. They make a map for her life.

Trix rides her luck. She reads the dice her own way. Whatever they say she decides what it means. Then she can do what she likes. This is the deal she has made with the dice. So they always fall out right.

Outside between stuttering streetlights a white van flickers in and out of sight. And then the street is empty. It leads to the end of town. It leads to a labyrinth of city after city. Each city is different, a different dream.

The street is empty. It leads to nowhere. Turns back on itself, again and again. Always bringing her here. Here where there is nothing. Here where she calls home.

Downstairs her mother is sleeping. She is dreaming of her daughter. A girl trapped in the light of a mirror, twisting the stem of an unused lipstick. Wearing the dress which sings in the wind. The dress which her own mother gave her. Which she never dared to wear.

Trix turns her back on the window. There is no window. There is no street. There is no room. The dice trickle lifeless from her fingers. Cursed by a birth sign which is not her own.

- 40 -

Trix shifts empty cups, the plastic spoons. The unwrapped sugar cubes. Backwards and forwards across the formica table top. A game of chess. The cafe feels crowded even when it's empty.

She strokes the cat that stalks languid as sunshine down from the counter. Then she gazes back to her tabletop chess, pushing the ashtray alongside the salt, manoeuvring the bottle of sauce.

The smell of slow coffee, the clatter of cups. A man crosses the floor to sit down next to her table in this room that's too small. He leans over and asks to borrow the sugar.

Trix looks away, it's not the words that count, it's the touch. But their fingers do not meet as she passes the bowl. No-one says anything, though the pulse of his voice awakes the nerve-ends under her skin, a radio wave alive in her brain.

As she turns back to her own table, a stem of unused lipstick clatters from her pocket and rolls across the floor. She watches its arcing journey, but lets it lie where it stops, next to the stranger's foot. Then with one hand she strokes the cat as it settles in the chair beside her. With the other she places a cigarette packet next to her empty cup.

They do not touch.

Another move.

It's just a game of chess.

- 41 -

Rafferty turns the corner. Cuts the engine. Turns on the radio. In the wing mirror kids play chicken-run, dodging late-night buses along the terraced streets. The air hangs heavy as weighted curtains in that silence after thunder. Gutters run swollen with dirty water, dragging cans and sodden paper to clog the crooked grids.

Across wasteland a man is dancing. He wears a hacked-open teddy bear like a hunter's pelt on his head. Stumbles through a maze of broken bricks without ever losing his footing. A girl with glasses like cats eyes is crossing through nettles towards him. She hesitates when she sees him, then twirls a majorette's baton, tossing it high to the dark night sky where it's suddenly picked out by the spotlight of the police helicopter hovering above them. Rotor blades whirl like an angry hornet as it watches while the couple dance towards each other, till they clutch in a clumsy waltz beside a burnt-out car.

They pirouette and bow as the helicopter soars away, leaving them suddenly in darkness as Rafferty's headlights leave them too.

He jerks the van to a halt and reverses. He's lost. No he's not - Rafferty's never lost. Just doesn't know where he is.

He turns on the radio.

"Block the dial... Unlock your eyes... Nobody sleeps from now till dawn..... Is there somebody there? Talk to me. Talk to me. Don't hang up."

She hangs up. Someone else lost too. Not in the city. Not in the street. In her own room. Lost for words. Lost for reasons. Lost.

Rafferty revs through a maze of streets. Each one looks the same. Turns the corner. He's back at the waste-ground again. Nearly hits a figure that he swears came from nowhere. Suddenly materialised out of the air. Out of his head. The van swerves and judders across the jarring waste-ground. Off the road.

There's no-one there.

No-one in the street. Not walking or standing or slumped in a heap. Just no-one at all. Dead air.

There's no-one there.

Rafferty sits at the wheel, shaken. His headlamps light on a ripped teddy bear and a majorette stick, hanging in the nettles. He turns the engine off. No light. On the radio, Max's voice is silent.

Searches the shadows between the streetlamps, looking for a figure. He could swear...

There's no-one there.

Rafferty props his head on the wheel.

He's asleep.

Across the waste-ground a tall figure glides. Stops by the van. Taps on the side window's misted glass. Peers in.

- 42 -

He maps by the stars. A dance across time. He wants to join the stars. Above him they are a mesh. He follows the paths which become a journey which takes him from street to street. But he is not in the streets. He is between the stars.

"What do you think about the situation?"

A wilting flower still drawls from his fingers, wasted now from waving all day at the people on buses where he sits at the crossroads. But they are not buses. They are not people. They are star travellers, just like he is, though they do not know it. He wishes them safe journey.

"What do you think about the situation?"

Street to street. Star to star. This city maps out universes.

There are no stars tonight but still he is not lost. There are other stars, other signs, and he follows, sometimes grubbing them up as he goes - in huge chubby fingers that still cling to the flowers. Bottle tops, beads, broken glass. All that glints. He clutches the pieces in his palm. A universe in his hand.

"What do you think about the situation?"

A path of crazy paving, crazy paving stones broken and stumbling. Stooping walls, nettles and dark bushes. A square where there used to be houses. He can feel them standing above him. The rooms, the walls. He feels their weight, but now they are no longer there. Only air. And a clear route to the stars.

Which are not there. It is dark. The stars have not come. But there are other stars. He holds them in his hand. All that glints. There are always other stars. He strews them before him so he can follow them again. Gleam and glisten in the darkness. Universes among the other universes. Tin cans, cats' eyes.

That's when he sees her. The frames of her glasses are like cats' eyes. She dances slow towards him. She clutches a majorette's stick. Tosses it high as the street lights above them. Which are not lit.

As the stars are not lit. Then they are hit by a light from the sky. A lightning bolt of energy. All the stars together. They dance for the stars. He takes her in his arms, this creature filled with wisdom whose eyes are windows to the universe.

He cradles her and rocks her, tranced in their spotlight. Lost and found, lost and found. Above them is a clatter like a thousand rooks and magpies. Squawking and wheeling. Stealing the sky.

And then the light is gone away. A helicopter skulks the space between them and the stars. Which are not there. Which are here. He holds them in his palm. He wants to give them to her, but when he looks there is nothing, they have gone. He doesn't know what to say.

"What do you think about the situation?"

Briefly, light returns. A van's dazed headlights, watching them. They pirouette and bow beside a burnt-out car. And then there is only darkness as the van reverses. Down streets from another map, merged into another journey.

- 43 -

Through the frame of her window, through the frame of his own, she sees him. Each time he turns his light on. Down there in the opposite block. Half way up. Half way down. She watches from up here. Each time he turns his light on. She turns her light off. All the better to see you with.

These eyes see. See it all. And she paints it on the wall. Frame by frame. Like a strip cartoon running round the room. She daubs the paint. As fast as she can, the colours dripping from the can across to the walls. Where she scrawls it all, over and over. His every movement.

That boy with the guitar on the seventh floor. She watches him hook up his Stratocaster, ram home the jack and run his fingers across the fretboard.

She picks sticks of charcoal, works in a frenzy, her fingers smeared till she uses them instead, a hazed smudge of fingerprints capturing the texture. Her own contribution to the flat's mosaic of history, posters and press-cuttings papered between the paper.

A painted rainbow frames the window which frames the frame where she sees him. Night after night, after day. She cannot hear him but she watches him play, unlocking the riff that aches inside him that she cannot hear. But she dances anyway. Dances to the music as she streaks her paint, wielding the brush like a majorette stick, the lines writhing with feeling.

She wants to be there with him. She wants the music to be hers. For it to fill her body, to well through her pores. Like the paint which clings there now as she rolls across the walls. Skin to paint, paint to plaster. Plaster to skin. Rubbing it in. She watches him. She is there. Gripped in his arms. But like a guitar. She is his music.

On the landing the wind is howling through the slats of the windows, up from the rubbish chute, clattering the letterboxes, lifting front door mats.

Down below, the caretaker scrubs graffiti off with a cloth, a lipstick scoreboard scrawled around the door.

- 44 -

She will come here. To this space. To this room. To this anywhere which is her own time in any place. Trix licks her lips. Places one knowing finger firmly between them. An ocean of energy grows restless inside her. She can feel its tides tugging her, this way, this way.

The room slopes away from her, out of her reach, an easy loping beat, drawing her out, twining her in, onwards towards an inevitable end.

There is a darkness inside her eyes, into which she swims. Glistening and beautiful she slips from her own embrace, sliding like a newborn child to walk as if naked in a crowded street where strangers will kiss her will touch her will love her, their faces like clowns like mirrors like masks, will breathe unspoken in her body's sunlit shadow.

There are voices in her fingertips, begging with her, pleading, drawing the darkness to dance across her skin, a curtain of satin, a veil of silk, washing her body with the sureness of milk.

And she cries out, the muted cry of a child, trapped behind her teeth, then vital and wild as she lets the sound roll, welling and bleeding to steal into corners, spreading warmth to this room.

And she touches the dust as the dust touches her, each shifting mote a skein of bright rainbows as out in the street warm rain soaks her skin as she dances beyond herself, arms reaching out, clutching the aura, gathering in.

To this room, to this space. To this anywhere which is her own time in any place. Here. She will come.

- 45 -

The sky is rising. She can feel it around her, leaving the ground on its journey to the sun. She longs to go with it.

She feels it gently lifting her limbs, as if she is bathing in air, her hair flowing softly behind her, her breath trapped within her, an ocean of energy.

The streets are peopled with glowing trees, reaching towards her, long arms stretching. Their fingers touch like clinging webs, pulling her back, pulling her back, but their soft warm voices lift her higher, whispering the words she has always known, which she has never heard before.

For the first time she sees the city below her, a map of rivers, of carnival tears. The music of dust, lost petals turning, through avenues of laughter, a fearless maze.

And at each open window the mothers of mothers, standing in a line behind their daughters, and their mothers too, waving and calling, sweet voices meshed with the waft of the trees.

She reaches upward. The clouds have gone. Now there is only the silence of wonder.

Only the sun.

- 46 -

Rafferty watches the washing on the line. A slow breeze. The washing on the line hangs almost still. Almost still as the cat which hangs at the top of the wall, only its tail tip twitching as it watches Rafferty watching the washing.

Blouses and bras, bras and blouses. And the lad's footie kit. And seven pairs of Rafferty's socks. Rafferty stretches and watches. This Donna likes to fold her sheets in the middle. But the other Donna likes to peg them at the end.

Rafferty has to remember. This Donna likes her veg on the left hand side, but the other Donna piles them on the right. Donna defrosts chicken in the microwave, but Donna leaves it out overnight.

Rafferty has to remember. But sometimes Rafferty forgets. Or sometimes he can't be bothered. And sometimes he forgets on purpose. And sometimes he thinks Donna likes that. He can tell by the way she giggles. A sort of welling spring that bubbles up inside her. But sometimes he thinks Donna's not so sure. And then he has to be careful.

The cat stretches carefully on the wall. Now the washing's hardly moving at all. Rafferty smiles at the way Donna and Donna both like to wash as many of his clothes as they can. Even if it's only the socks. Sort of like a trophy, just to prove that he's there. Or maybe when he's gone to show that he's not.

Till in the end there was all of them anyway.

Rafferty and Donna and Carla and Lee: and
Rafferty and Donna and Carla and Lee.

Donna and Donna. It's not hard to remember. Sheets and vegetables, chickens and socks. It's only like sisters after all. Rafferty shrugs - and he's always had plenty of those - as the cat slinks slowly away off the wall.

- 47 -

Empty kitchen. Her mother's at work and her father's gone out. Unwashed plates on the table. She fishes a half-smoked cigarette from the ashtray and lights it. Stubs it out again.

Trix sits and looks at the photo of her mother next to the radio, next to the clock. She never wants to be like her. So she paints her face, she wears clothes she knows her mother would never wear. She is rewriting her life, every day like a page from a diary. Slow motion music runs backward. Every night is packed with action.

As if. Like this.

In the cupboard the wrapper of a loaf with two dry slices still left inside it. Scraping of margarine in a plastic tub.

Trix lights the grill and rereads the headlines on last night's paper, spreading it out across the table, pushing the plates and the dishes aside.

The toast burns. She opens the fridge. There's no milk left for the tea.

Trix sips black coffee and dreams. Kaleidescope streets. Lovers and winos. The blind penny whistle man plays fountains of colour. Strangers stop and touch each other.

In the cafes the revellers all wear photographs of themselves incase they forget who they are. Then a girl comes in, looking ill, looking thin, her face overshadowed by long heavy earrings, and gives her picture away to the man standing next to her. He gives her his in return. And everyone exchanges until nobody's got their own picture anymore, and nobody knows who they are.

And when the warm wind calls they all dance into the streets, looking for each other again.

- 48 -

Under the old bridge. Watching the sunrise through a broken window. City sounds creep cold. Waking whispers.

Skyline of lives piled high on each other. In drunken doorways and lonely basements the day's grey journeys wait.

Kissing shadows. Car wheels hiss. Soundtrack stutters a nervous pulse. Night jives die. Tired lives hidden inside pale eyes. Taking the days. A calendar of capsules. Swallowing lies.

A tall man rises from the steps of the basement and wraps the coat around his shoulders. Not for warmth, not for protection. His skin feels the rain like grains of dirt. Only for disguise from the watching eyes. Which do not see him.

He sips black coffee in the shadowy corner of an early morning cafe. Watches himself in the window's slant reflection, but nobody notices. Nobody sees him. But he sees them. The precision of dust on the picture rail. The colour of the pool player's eyes.

His cup is empty. He places it in the exact centre of the table, relaxes in the corner seat. From here he can watch the room, watch the street. Fragile eyes. He stares through walls, through each mesh of conspiracy.

She is in the street again. Big rings glint on her fingers for luck. Her teeth are tainted when she smiles.

He feels her sit beside him, though she has taken her place in the garage across the road. Behind the glass.

Behind the till. The forecourt cracked and webbed with weeds.

She watches the long cars come and go. Drive in, fill up. Give her the money, wait for the change. Different faces, different cars. Nobody ever speaks to her. She never sees them again.

But she would lay her whole life out for one glass of brandy. Tell all and nothing at all between the courses of a candlelit supper.

He takes her hand right there at the table as she ravels out her story of how she's a long lost Hollywood queen.

She changes her name each time she tells it. He understands. But she really was there. Her own name limps in on the tail-end of the credits on a string of B-movies.

And each stranger she talks to is another bit-part scene. Her name at the end of every reel, her name. Counting the frames, her face glistening next to the stars. Check out the hat-check girls, and bar-room cuties, the chorus line, the bathing beauties.

She was there. She was there. And to prove it, she's here. Here she is. With her name at the end. At the end.

The end.

- 49 -

Last night's thunder still lurks about the block, heavy and humid, trapped between landings, rattling in the lift, glowering in the stairwell.

Albie tries to sweep it out, to douse its stench from the rubbish chute; to sluice it with buckets of dull bleached water as it clings to slippery handrails with its sleepless fingernails and sits in still dark doorways coughing gouts of blood and bile.

A backwash of sour rain, sullen and muddied, recedes across the floor of the entrance hall. Albie jams the double doors open, hoping the heat will just drain away as he stands and watches a gang of young lads playing football by the garages. Hair plastered flat to their foreheads by a mixture of sweat and persistent thin drizzle, so fine they can hardly see it.

- 50 -

As she gets off the bus she lights another cigarette. She tries to light another cigarette. Her fingers fumble its shape to her mouth. Jabbing it between the red of her lips. The matches slip as she tries to strike one. The flame goes out, blown out by the slipstream fumes of the bus as it retreats down the street.

She doesn't know where she is. The street is dark. The lamps are broken, unlit. Watching. She knows when someone is watching. Someone is watching her now. But nobody is here. An empty street.

She strikes a match. She lights her cigarette. Clings to it like a stick. For protection. To guide her. Its glowing tip the only light as its ash spills down her dress.

"The sky's full of rain... I can feel it in my head... in a cloud shaped like pain..."

The pain has led her here. She is not in the room where the pain lives with her. Beside the empty bed where she never sleeps.

"It's cold... and it's dark... so I don't want to go out... so I get on the bus... okay?...... OKAY."

But the bus has gone. Its lights have gone. Its warmth has gone. The other passengers who looked at her but did not look at her. Were there. But are not here now. Nobody here now. But someone is watching her. She can feel the eyes. She knows. Most people do not want to see her. Look away. Or they stare. And she knows. Now no-one is here, but she knows.

The road slopes away. Uneven paving stones. Slipping between the terraced houses, down towards the river. Waiting like a darkness, like a stillness at the bottom of the hill. She cannot see it, but she knows it's there. Can feel its tug. Feel that chill. Maybe it's only the river that watches. She shrugs, shivering, going that way. But no, she knows. There is someone else. Not eyes behind the curtains. They don't count, they are always there. No, there's someone else there, out here, with her. Someone in this street.

She stops. Her feet miss a beat. Are those the echoes of other footsteps? Is someone keeping time with her? She turns to look. A swirl of smoke from her cigarette's stub. There's no-one here.

Distant sirens. A riverboat's moan.

She hugs herself. She would like someone to. Someone to hold her. Anyone would do. Just to be held. She looks again. Her eyes pulse pain, like the pain in her head. She smudges red lips with the back of her sleeve.

In the doorway, in the darkness, where there is no-one, where there is nothing. There is someone there.

He does not surprise her. She is not startled. She always knows when someone is watching. But she did not expect the eyes. The eyes that see her without seeing her. Which look at her and through her and do not see.

But see everything.

And she wasn't expecting the touch of his body. So moist, so warm. Like a day-old baby, but fully grown.

Wrapped in long darkness. Like a cloak, like a coat. To protect them. As they dance, in the silence, in the darkness.

He takes her to another place. She does not know where she is now, though she did not know where she was before. They dance through darkness, through hidden walls. Through gardens of light, to and fro, to and fro, feeling the salt, the oil, the flow, till her skin seems to glow.

They dance through cities beneath this city, where sunken rivers run.

They go there.

He takes her.

She is not alone.

- 51 -

No-one says anything. Their guitars become their tongues. Handle them like weapons, like lovers, like sons. The frets played smooth, the paint worn away. Sunburst and jet, matted with dust. The strings jangle rust.

Tune up like they're clearing their throats. One by one they plug in, cut the air with their riffs. Age old arguments wrangle across time. They don't know what they're doing here but there's no going back, so they're stuck with each other. Out of place. Out of time. Edgy and tetchy.

"What're we waiting for?" somebody mutters.

"Waiting for Rafferty."

"Everyone always waited for him.

Biographies

Dave Ward's poems have been published widely in magazines and anthologies; and broadcast on television and radio. He was visiting writer in residence at Nanyang University, Singapore and has toured to Hong Kong and northern China. Previous collections include Jambo (Paul Weller's Riot Stories Ltd), On the Edge of Rain (Headland) and, writing as David Greygoose, he is the author of Brunt Boggart (Hawkwood/Pushkin).

Bryan Biggs' drawings have been shown in several exhibitions including the Jerwood Drawing Prize and in publications such as Smoke, The Drawing Paper and Responses: Intercultural Drawing Practice (cair, Liverpool School of Art and Design). Since 2018 he has done a drawing every day.